Linda's Lie

Linda's Lie

Bernard Ashley

Illustrated by Janet Duchesne

Julia MacRae Books

A division of Franklin Watts

Text © 1982 Bernard Ashley
Illustrations © 1982 Janet Duchesne
All rights reserved
First published in Great Britain 1982 by
Julia MacRae Books
A division of Franklin Watts Ltd.
12a Golden Square, London W1R 4BA
and Franklin Watts Inc.
387 Park Avenue South, New York 10016.

Reprinted 1984

British Library Cataloguing in Publication Data
  Ashley, Bernard
  Linda's lie—(Blackbirds)
  I. Title
  823′.914[J] PZ7

ISBN 0–86203–099–4 UK edition
ISBN 0–531–04576–5 US edition
Library of Congress Catalog No. 82–81792

Phototypeset by Ace Filmsetting Ltd., Frome, Somerset
Made and printed in Great Britain by Camelot Press, Southampton

Chapter 1

"What's that school playing at? Don't they know there's no pound pieces here to spare for *outings*?" Mr. Steel said the word as if it tasted bad in his mouth.

Linda looked up at his stern, black face, at the eyes which were telling a different story to the mouth. Her father smacked his knee with the flat of his hand. She knew that sign. He was just as angry with himself for not having the money to spare.

But still she said it. She wanted him to know all the facts before they threw a cover over the whole idea, like putting the yellow canary to sleep for the night. "It's the ballet," she said, "*The Sleeping Beauty* in a theatre. That's why it's a pound."

"I'll do you a dance for sixpence, girl." He smiled: but once more his

eyes and his mouth were at odds.

"The letter says see Miss if it's hardship over money . . ."

She thought his head was going to hit the ceiling. "Hardship over money? *Hardship over money*? Sweet Lord, I'll give your Miss 'hardship over money'! Does she know there's no money to go looking for work some mornings? Does she know your brother needs new shoes, your mattress can't be fit for a dog to lie on, your mam and me's fed up to kingdom come with the taste of jam—and she wants to take you to the ballet! Hardship over money is right—but you don't catch me asking favours for that my girl. That don't come into it, no way!"

He pushed out of the door and thumped up the stairs to the bathroom—while the canary screeched in fright and seed went flying all over.

Linda climbed onto a chair and pulled the cover over the bird. "There!" she said. "Now shut up— 'cos that's that!" And on flat feet she went to find her mam, all that walking on her toes forgotten.

4

Chapter 2

Linda didn't really know how to tell Miss Smith. She knew her teacher wanted all of them to go, and she knew the school had money for the ones who couldn't afford it. Which meant Miss Smith would be upset if Linda's parents didn't want to ask for it.

"Don't you *want* to go, Linda?" she'd ask. "I always thought you were so keen." How could she tell her that her daddy didn't think it was important? That would be like saying something against Miss Smith.

The other trouble was, it was always done in the open—all in the classroom where the others could hear. Wouldn't Donna Paget make a meal of it? A fuss like that. And Jason Paris? He could squash you down with something he said as easy as he squashed other people's plasticine.

No. She'd have to find some other excuse. She was going to have to tell Miss Smith a lie.

In the classroom Monday morning all the money was starting to come in. There were pounds here and pounds there, some held out on palms like sports day medals and others clutched tight like family jewels. Even Jason Paris had his, a handful of heavy silver in tens, clunking on the table top.

Linda's name came halfway down the girls. Most times people were getting noisy by then—but today they were as quiet as mice.

"Linda Steel?"

"Please, Miss, I'm not going, Miss." Linda felt bad already, and she was only telling the truth so far.

Miss Smith looked up at her, surprised. Across the other side Donna Paget coughed, or something.

"You're not going, Linda? Oh dear. Why ever not?" For a second or two she sat waiting for the reason: then she must have guessed it could be awkward. "Come up here, love."

Linda went out to the front. Everyone stared. It was still so quiet she felt like a dancer about to do one of the hard bits.

"Please, Miss," Linda said,

stopping and taking a deep breath, getting close enough to smell the teacher's hair. "I've got to go to a christening."

"Really? On a Monday?"

"I think it's special," she said in a low voice. She looked at Miss Smith. She was nodding.

Lying was easier than she thought. All you had to do was say it.

"Well, they can't change that, I suppose. And we can't change the day, either. What a shame—and you're one of my best dancers."

Linda smiled a brave, sad smile which said all she needed. A lie smile. That was easy, too.

"What church is that, then?" Donna Paget asked at playtime. Donna had very good ears, Linda thought—or else she could *see* what people said.

"Somewhere up London. A special one. They have their Sundays on Mondays."

"That's silly. Never heard of that before."

"Well, you have now, haven't you?"

"Who's it being christened?"

"My uncle," Linda said. She didn't know what made her say it, what made the lie get bigger. But she had heard of grown-ups having it done—and this day did have to be a bit special.

Donna Paget crossed her legs the way her mother did when she busted her sides. "They'll have a job lifting him up for the water bit," she laughed.

Linda stared her out. "He's not very heavy," she answered.

But she knew that was wrong. The whole thing was going wrong already—and she'd only just started the lie.

Chapter 3

Mr. Steel came away from the window and crackled the envelope in his fingers. He walked past the end of the out-of-work line and found a hard bench to sit on. Carefully, he opened what he had in his hand. When he hadn't earned it, it hardly seemed his to touch, let alone his to risk tearing. But he counted it, the notes and the jangle of coins which came last.

He sighed. There was a use for it all, and none left over. Shaking his head, he turned up his collar and went out. It was a long walk home when you had to pretend the buses weren't going your way.

But the buses going past weren't passing just him. With all the rest of the traffic they were skimming past a stranded car at the side of the road. The car rocked with the buffeting of air, and the man who was bent over by the wheel was swearing.

"Blessed garages!" he said, throwing the wheel-brace into the kerb. "They don't think someone might have to undo these blessed nuts!"

Mr. Steel stopped. He knew the

problem. Garages put the wheel-
nuts on with special tools, and
getting them off when you had a
puncture was murder.

"Stupid little wheel-brace!" the
man was saying. "It's got no *push*."

The man was in a suit, but his
hands and face were grimy with car
dirt.

Mr. Steel stopped. "Let's have a
go, mate. See if a fresh pair of
hands can do it."

The man looked hard at Mr.
Steel and picked up the wheel-brace.
"Thanks a lot," he said.

Mr. Steel took a firm grip and
pulled, and pushed. But he couldn't
shift any of the nuts on his own.

14

"Give it a go together," he said,
rubbing his hands and drawing
breath.

They had to hug to do it. Hands
just fitting side by side on the wheel-
brace, arms round each other's
waists. Cheek to cheek, black and
white, breathing in each other's

breath, they one-two-three'd, and strained, and arched . . . and shifted the first nut. And then the other three.

"Phew! Thanks a lot, mate. I'm very grateful to you." He pushed an oily hand into his pocket and pulled out a pound piece. "You'll have a drink with me, won't you?"

Mr. Steel looked at the man. Don't spoil it by offering me money, his eyes seemed to say. And then they seemed to think of something else.

"All right, friend, I will." He took the coin. "Good health," he said.

"Cheers," said the man. "You saw me out of trouble, there."

16

Chapter 4

At home, the last thing Linda
wanted was any talk of ballet, or
dancing, or theatres. Even school
seemed a dangerous subject to get
on. She didn't want her father
angry about the outing, or sorry.
She didn't want her mother taking
her side or her brother Michael
asking questions. She had started
something off—something bad—
and all she wanted now was for next
Monday to come and go with
nothing said.

She'd have liked to hibernate till Tuesday. But she couldn't do that. She had to stew inside, and act normal.

That evening she sat in front of the television in dread of *Blue Peter* doing a bit about the ballet. Or of Michael kicking his leg over the chair arm and asking whose room she'd go in when her class was out. She didn't want him looking for her in school that day.

What did you do out of school all day anyway? Someone could see you—even your father, when he was out looking for work!

Her heart turned over when he came in. It was horrible. She wasn't pleased to see him. She had to act it. Is this what being a liar's like? she thought. This nasty pain all the time, and not being able to look straight at your dad?

And he seemed all full of himself today—taller in the doorway. But he didn't say why, not to her, nor to Michael. He looked at the TV set, hummed a little something deep in his throat and went out to the kitchen.

It was bed-time before Linda found out what it was. And then it wasn't her father who told her. He wasn't a showy man.

"Look!" said her mother as she tucked Linda in on the lumpy mattress. She held out a shiny pound piece. "This is for your outing. Your daddy got it extra today. Did a little job for a man he met. We won't miss it, being extra." She was smiling such a happy smile.

Linda looked up at the coin. It should have looked good and made her smile, but it didn't. It looked like money from another country. Even the Queen looked cross as if she was saying, "We've found you out, Linda Ann Steel. Look where lying leads you . . ."

Linda's eyes filled with tears. She put her head under the blankets to hide them—and she suddenly felt like their silent canary must feel— covered, and trapped: only she was in a cage of lies.

"Ah—don't cry, Petal." Her mother patted the mound of her head. "It's a happy ending to the story, eh?"

Chapter 5

The cold coin in Linda's sock seemed to stick out like some nasty bite. You could see it if you knew where to look for it, even with white socks on. And you'd see where it had been when she took them off for dance, grazing her all grey where it scratched her ankle.

But she didn't know what else to do with it. She couldn't just give it in and say she was going to the ballet after all. Not really. They didn't cancel christenings just like that, and she'd made it sound much too important to just have changed her mind.

There was nowhere to hide it at home where someone wouldn't come across it—and nobody's place was secret enough in school. The only other thing would be to throw it away. But she shivered at the thought. A picture in her head of her father working for it made the money much too precious for that.

It weighed her down as if it had been in pennies. Why had she had to tell Miss Smith a lie? It had seemed easy at first, but now it was getting harder and harder every minute.

With her bag held against her leg

she went into the classroom. Today she really didn't want to be at school. But if she thought things were bad there was worse to come. Life could play some terrible tricks.

"Listen, children, I've got something important to ask you. Andrew Field has lost his ballet money. He thinks he left it in his bag in the cloakroom—silly boy—but he's just been back to look, and it isn't there."

Everyone looked at Andrew Field, mouths in little O's. He put on a tragic face and stared at his *Happy Reader*. Then they looked for Jason Paris: but he was late again. He'd kick his way into the classroom in a minute—in a mood, but innocent!

"Mind you, Andrew could have dropped it somewhere else. So if anyone comes across it I'll be very grateful."

Linda remembered past fusses about missing things. A feeling of nobody being trusted would hang in the classroom till the money was found, or it was forgotten.

"Anyway, it's our hall time now, so let's get changed for it quickly and quietly."

Now Linda had to take her socks off. And just as she knew it would, the pound piece in the right one seemed to burn like something jumped out from a bonfire. If anyone saw that now it would be much too late to say she'd brought her money to go after all. There'd be all sorts of questions asked, and Donna Paget would think it was Christmas. They'd have to talk to her parents to clear it up, and then all the christening lie would come out.

"Hurry up, Linda. Come on, it's not like you to be slow for dance."

But getting off a sock with money

in it was every bit as difficult as
Linda thought it would be. The
hard-edged lump kept riding up
with her leg and seemed to want to
jump itself out and onto the floor.
And trapping it between her thumb
and her sock only left that guilty
secret showing in her hand.

There was only one last chance.
She pretended the sock was too
tight and did the other one instead.
If she hid the money leg, she told
herself, she could do it while the

others went out of the room.

She pulled her dress over her head, folded it with the one sock hidden, and sat up straight with her arms on the desk. Ready. The whole room was ready.

"Good." Miss Smith stood up.

"Please, Miss, Linda Steel's left one sock on!" Donna Paget sounded as if she'd discovered a new planet. And everyone laughed as if it was the best joke ever invented. Even Andrew Field forgot he was supposed to be worried sick about his money.

Linda closed her eyes. Tight, dry, guilty eyes.

"Come on," said Miss Smith.

"Silly girl. Clocks won't stop for you." She hurried in a zig-zag between the tables. "Cock your leg up."

There was nothing else Linda could do. She was done for. Inside she had that empty, helpless feeling of just going off under gas at the dentist's. She felt Miss Smith lift her foot, and she thought she heard her own voice saying something beginning with "I . . ." She could hear the class laughing at the sight of Miss Smith helping her. But no noise was loud enough to cover the sound of the pound as its hard, ringing edge hit the floor.

"Whee, Miss . . ."

"Linda Steel!"

"Hey, look, Andrew . . ."

Public shock. Private glee. Even good friends drew in their breath.

"I think you'd better take this money and have a little talk with Mrs. Cheff, Linda," said Miss Smith. "Don't you?"

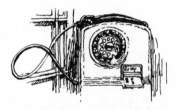

Chapter 6

It was a cold and windy morning
but Mr. Steel forced himself to be up
and out at his old time for work. It
did no good to let things slide.
Besides, there was something special
he had to do before he could rest
easy in his mind.

He went to the end of the street
and pulled himself into the telephone
box. In a few moments—using the
phone as an ear-muff against the
icy blast coming through a broken
pane—he was talking to Linda's

headmistress.

"It's a jolly good job you phoned," Mrs. Cheff told him after hearing what he wanted. "Linda's not down as going, not on the list. She said something about going to a christening."

Mr. Steel frowned. It was a bad line and the cold wind was howling. It had almost sounded like *christening*, what the headmistress had said. "No, it's the dancing she wants. I give her the money, only it was late and I was scared the seats had all run out."

"Really, they get so muddled!" Mrs. Cheff complained. "And they seem to think money grows on trees, don't they?"

Mr. Steel didn't answer. That bit didn't sound like Linda.

"I'll find out why she hasn't paid. I'm sure we've still got a seat. I just hope she hasn't lost the money."

"So do I," said Mr. Steel. "So do I." And shaking his head he put the phone back on its cold cradle.

Chapter 7

Mrs. Cheff took Linda into her
room. She sat in her swivel chair
and looked at the red-eyed girl.
"Really, Linda! You do seem to
have lost your senses. How could you
be so stupid with someone else's
money?"

Linda's toes curled into the
flattened carpet. She frowned at
Mrs. Cheff's knees. Everything had
got out of hand so quickly. She
didn't know what to do, what to say.
If she told Mrs. Cheff the truth,

what would her father say about the lie? But, then, what would he say about them thinking she'd stolen somebody's pound?

"It's just as well the pound turned up, isn't it?"

Linda stared at Mrs. Cheff. But she kept her mouth shut tight. How

did she know about the money down her sock? Miss Smith hadn't told her—she'd left that to Linda. Could she see through the wall or something, like she always said she could?

"Your father phoned—sensible man—so I knew you had a pound to pay. No thanks to you, Linda, was it?"

Linda shook her head. He'd phoned? Then Mrs. Cheff knew she was supposed to go. That meant she knew she wasn't a thief. But it also meant she'd found out about the lie!

"Although I still don't know why you said you were going to a christening. Your father didn't seem to understand either. Unless it was something to do with what we're going to see. *The Sleeping Beauty*. Was it some silly joke about seeing the baby's christening on the stage?"

It went very quiet in the small room. Linda heard the sounds of music from the hall and wished she were there with the rest of the class.

She looked at her feet. So Mrs. Cheff thought she'd said something clever about the ballet to Miss Smith—a joke, not a lie.

She wanted to nod. She could easily nod and keep quiet, she thought. Nothing needed to be said. That would leave the whole thing sorted out.

But Mrs. Cheff didn't give her time to work out what to do. "What I don't understand most of all, though, is how you could think a whole pound piece was so *unimportant*. Fancy not telling us about it! A pound was a pound in my day, you know."

What was that? *Unimportant*? Linda's stare was sore, and shocked. Mrs. Cheff could say what she liked about stealing or lying—but no-one in her house thought a pound piece was *unimportant*! She knew the worth of a pound better than Mrs. Cheff did. And that pound had been worth ten to her father. For his sake she couldn't keep quiet about that.

"I wasn't being stupid with that money, Miss. I was *hiding* it. I didn't drop it down a drain, did I?"

"Didn't drop it down a drain?"

But now Linda was crying, and telling it all. In a thin, sobbing voice she was pouring out the whole story: all about her not going to the ballet at first, and the reason; and the lie to Miss Smith; and the mix-up over Andrew Field's money, and the pound down her sock.

At the end she took a deep breath and thrust out her hand with the hot pound in it.

Mrs. Cheff looked hard at it, and swivelled to pick up another pound piece from her desk. She frowned, then her face seemed to clear.

"I *see*," she said. "Then this isn't yours at all. It's Andrew Field's. I found it after your father phoned, in the cloakroom—rolled behind the door. He's the careless one. This is the money I was on about."

Linda's shoulders heaved in another sob. But it was the last. It had been good to clear everything up.

"Well, thank you for telling me,

Linda." She gave her arm a squeeze. "I'm very glad you did. It was important, wasn't it?" She gave her a pat on the head. "Now you'd better get back to lessons. You're missing your chance to dance."

Linda couldn't trust herself to say thank you. She hurried out to find the others in the hall, her eyes still red, but with a new, smooth feeling inside.

Miss Smith must have told them to say no more, because no-one even looked at her. She stood in the doorway, listening. The music was beautiful, the sort that lifted the heart.

She glided into it with a lightness and a joy that only she could know about—like a happy bird with the cover off, suddenly released to dance free in the sky.